For Cynthia Leitich Smith and Dianna Hutts Aston—M. M.
For Kevin Lewis—K. C.

SIMON & SCHUSTER BOOKS FOR YOUNG READERS • An imprint of Simon & Schuster Children's Publishing Division • 1230 Avenue of the Americas, New York, New York 10020 • Text copyright © 2010 by Michelle Meadows • Illustrations copyright © 2010 by Kurt Cyrus • All rights reserved, including the right of reproduction in whole or in part in any form. • SIMON & SCHUSTER BOOKS FOR YOUNG READERS is a trademark of Simon & Schuster, Inc. • For information about special discounts for bulk purchases, please contact Simon & Schuster Special Sales at 1-866-506-1949 or business@simonandschuster.com. The Simon & Schuster Speakers Bureau can bring authors to your live event. For more information or to book an event, contact the Simon & Schuster Speakers Bureau at 1-866-248-3049 or visit our website at www.simonspeakers.com. • Book design by Chloë Foglia • The text for this book is set in Paradigm • The illustrations for this book are rendered in pencil with digital color. • Manufactured in China 1009 SCP • 10 9 8 7 6 5 4 3 2 1 • Library of Congress Cataloging-in-Publication Data • Meadows, Michelle. • Hibernation station / Michelle Meadows; illustrated by Kurt Cyrus. • p. cm. • Summary: Rhyming text and pictures introduce the reader to a variety of animals as they try to snuggle in to sleep. • ISBN: 978-1-4169-3788-3 (hardcover) • [1. Stories in rhyme. 2. Animals—Fiction. 3. Sleep—Fiction.] • I. Cyrus, Kurt, ill. • II. Title. • PZ8.3.M4625Hi 2010 • [E]—dc22 • 2008042141

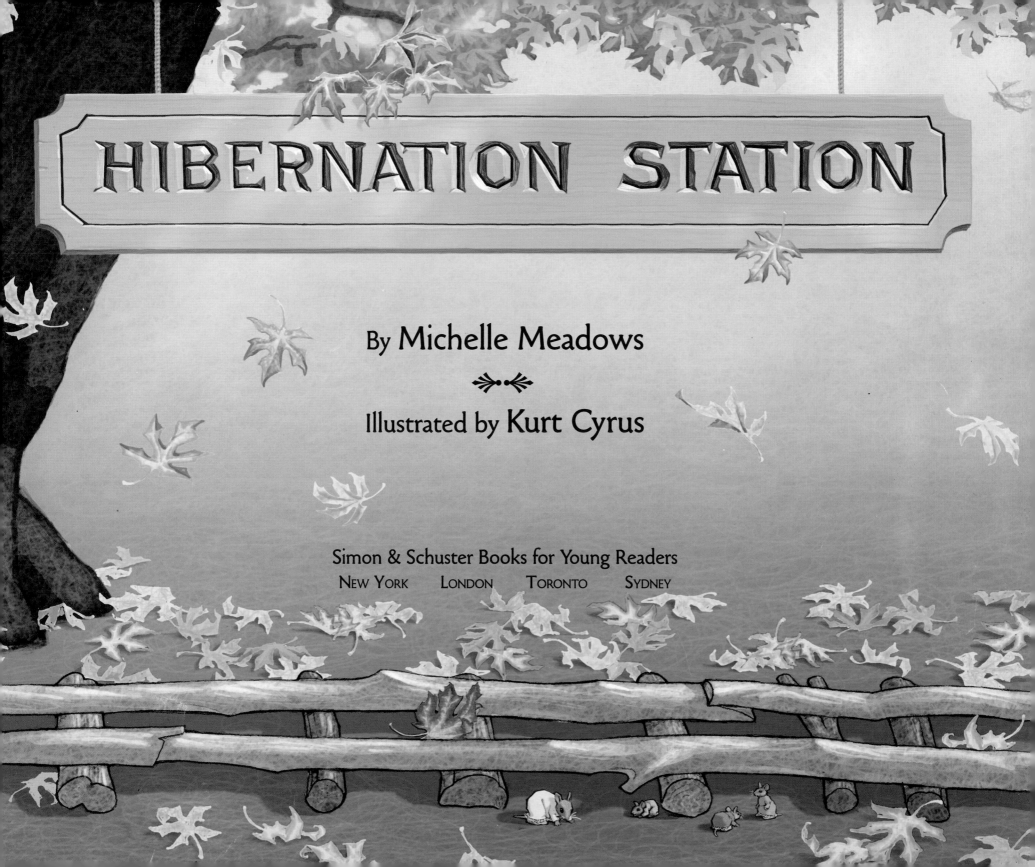

HIBERNATION STATION

By Michelle Meadows

Illustrated by Kurt Cyrus

Simon & Schuster Books for Young Readers
NEW YORK   LONDON   TORONTO   SYDNEY

Fuzzy slippers, warm pajamas.
Forest babies and their mamas . . .

show up early at the station!
Time for winter hibernation.

Bats and chipmunks in the middle.
Bears and mice, from big to little.

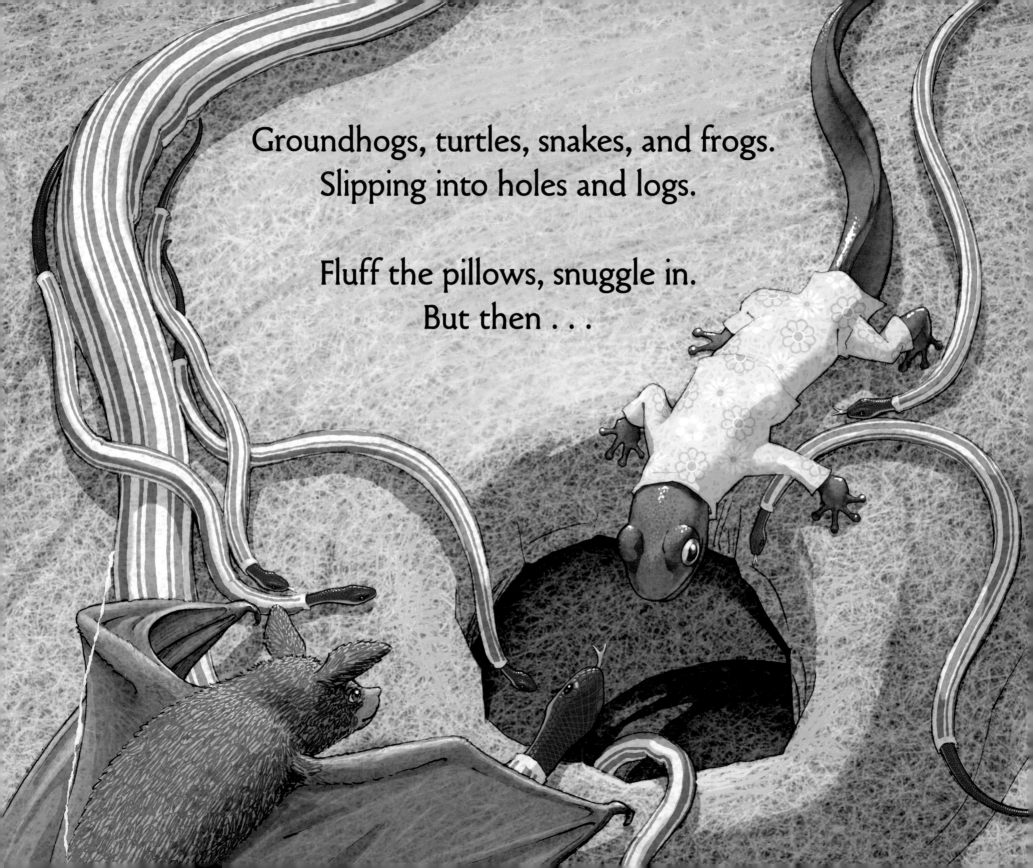

Groundhogs, turtles, snakes, and frogs.
Slipping into holes and logs.

Fluff the pillows, snuggle in.
But then . . .

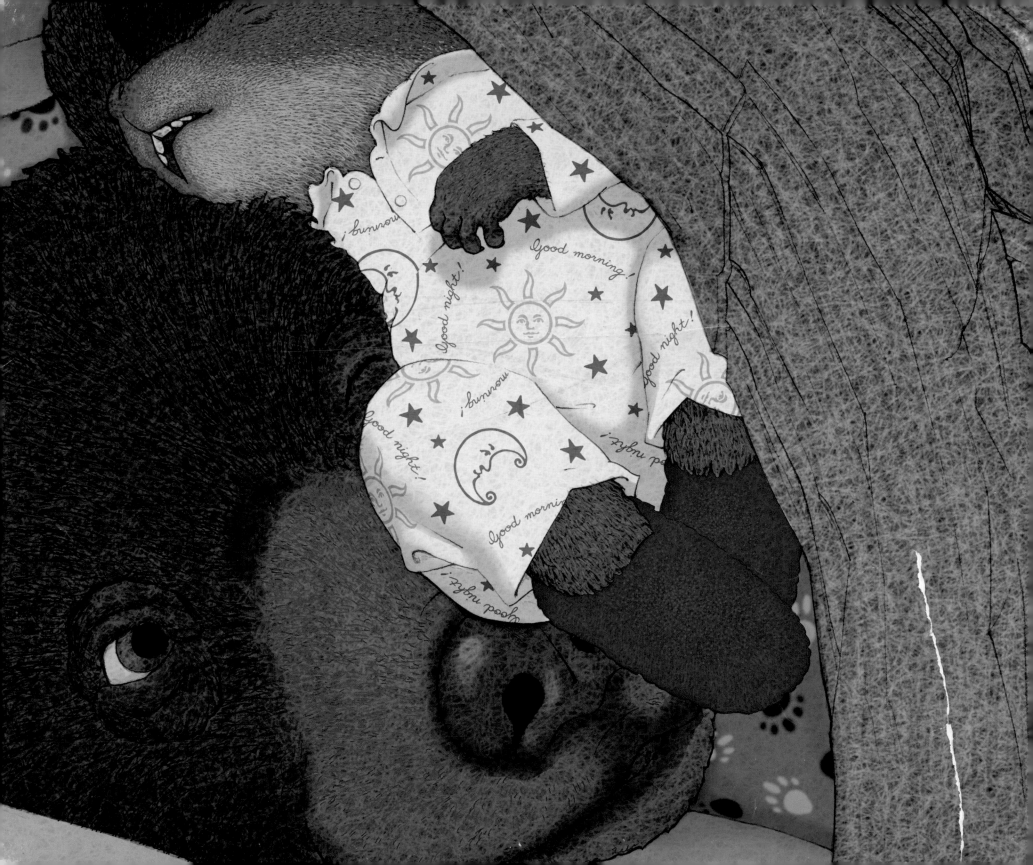

commotion in a den!

"I cannot sleep!" a black bear roars.

"My roommate rolls around and snores!"

A groundhog cries,
"This hole's too tight."

Then *uh-oh*—trouble near the stream.

The hedgehog babies start to scream!

Just when the beds begin to sink,
two chipmunks cry, "We spilled a drink!"

"And while you're up, we need more snacks.
And bring more pillows for our backs."

Just then, a frog begins to moan.
"I'm scared to be down here alone!"

The bears in charge (in railroad caps)
review the hibernation maps. . . .

C'mon, black bear! Bring your shoes.
Here's a quiet place to snooze.

C'mon, hedgehogs! Warm and dry.

Let's huddle for a lullaby.

C'mon, chipmunks! *Sip, sip, sip.*
Nibble, nibble. Drip, drip, drip.

Blankets, pillows, extra snug.
C'mon, frog! You need a hug.

Climb on top and join the heap.

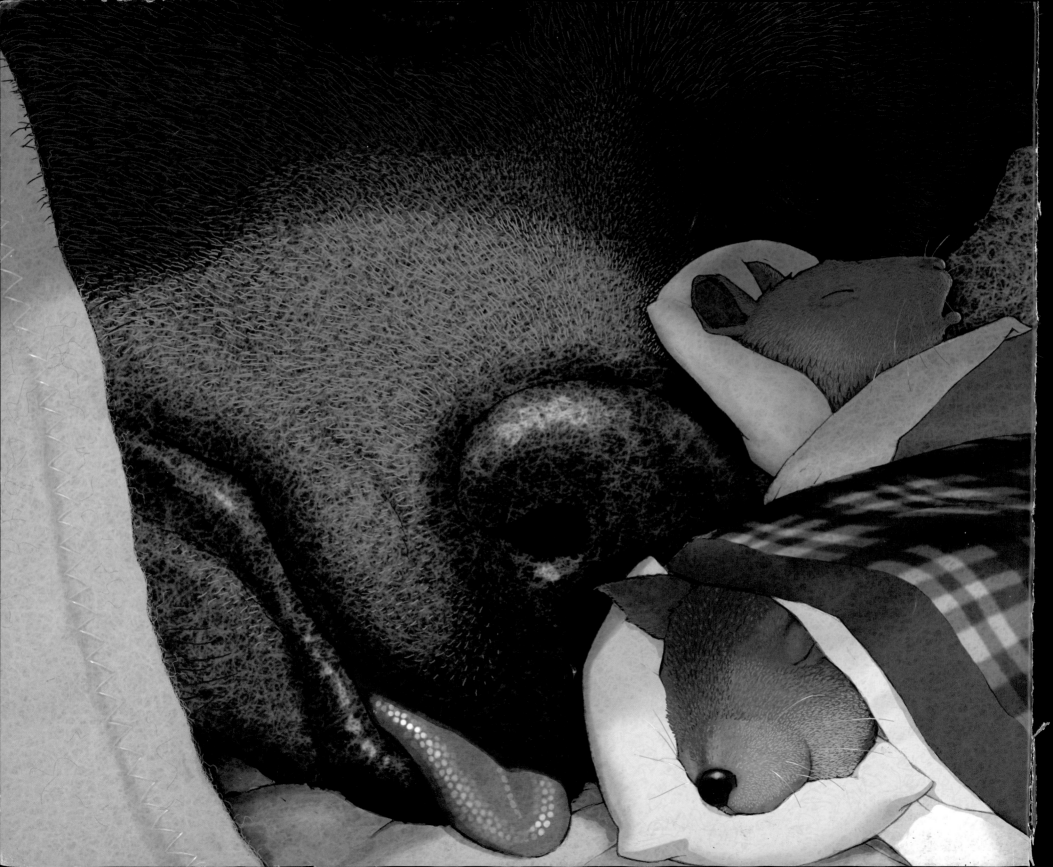

Soon everyone is fast asleep.

❧ Author's Note ❧

Hibernation is a fascinating way that some animals are able to survive during winter when food becomes scarce. Hibernation is commonly defined as a sleep-like state. To prepare for hibernation, some animals store food to eat periodically when they awaken, while others build up enough body fat so that they are able to sleep all winter. Some scientists say that there are varying degrees of hibernation. For example, "true hibernators" experience a dramatic drop in body temperature, heart rate, and breathing. These animals, sometimes called "deep sleepers," are hard to wake up in winter: examples are bats and groundhogs (also known as woodchucks). Other animals, known as "light sleepers," are easier to wake up: examples are raccoons and skunks. While not considered "true hibernators," they get sluggish in the winter and often curl up in groups to sleep.